BEAST QUEST

THE DARK REALM

⤙ BOOK EIGHTEEN ⤚

STING
THE SCORPION MAN

ADAM BLADE

ILLUSTRATED BY EZRA TUCKER

SCHOLASTIC INC.

New York Toronto London Auckland
Sydney Mexico City New Delhi Hong Kong

With special thanks to Lucy Courtenay

To Anna McCullough

No part of this work may be reproduced, stored in a retrieval system, or transmitted in any form or by any means, electronic, mechanical, photocopying, recording, or otherwise, without written permission of the publisher. For information regarding permission, write to Working Partners Ltd., Stanley House, St Chad's Place, London WC1X 9HH, United Kingdom.

ISBN 978-0-545-20036-3

Beast Quest series created by Beast Quest Ltd., London.
BEAST QUEST is a trademark of Beast Quest Ltd.

Published by Scholastic Inc., 557 Broadway, New York, NY 10012, by arrangement with Working Partners Ltd.
SCHOLASTIC and associated logos are trademarks and/or registered trademarks of Scholastic Inc.

12 11 10 9 8 7 6 5 4 3 2 1   11 12 13 14 15 16/0

Designed by Tim Hall
Printed in the U.S.A.
First printing, February 2011

40

Welcome. You stand on the edge of darkness, at the gates of an awful land. This place is Gorgonia, the Dark Realm, where the sky is red, the water black, and Malvel rules. Tom and Elenna — your hero and his companion — must travel here to complete the next Beast Quest.

Gorgonia is home to six most deadly Beasts — Minotaur, Winged Stallion, Sea Monster, Gorgonian Hound, Mighty Mammoth, and Scorpion Man. Nothing can prepare Tom and Elenna for what they are about to face. Their past victories mean little. Only strong hearts and determination will save them now.

Dare you follow Tom's path once more? I advise you to turn back. Heroes can be stubborn and adventures may beckon, but if you decide to stay with Tom, you must be brave and fearless. Anything less will mean certain doom.

Watch your step. . . .

Kerlo the Gatekeeper

THE **G**ORGONIAN **MEDICINE WOMAN TWITCHED** and muttered in her sleep. Her dreams were strange tonight.

A boy stood alone in a dark tunnel, his face bloody and streaked with sweat. In his hand was a battered wooden shield with six tokens embedded in its surface. Torches flickered along the passageway, throwing the boy's shadow onto the wall, where it stood huge and alone.

The boy was suddenly dwarfed by a second silhouette — a Beast with a sweeping tail and monstrous pincers that snipped and slashed at the air.

A giant scorpion!

The medicine woman moaned in her sleep as

the silhouette grew clearer. The creature was more than a scorpion. It was half man!

The boy whirled around, raising his sword, as the Beast attacked with his razor-sharp pincers.

"Tom!"

A girl's voice screamed. It was Elenna, the girl the medicine woman had helped to heal. She stood with a wolf by her side, and held a bow with an arrow in the bowstring. She let the arrow fly at the scorpion, but it bounced harmlessly off the creature's body. The boy stumbled and the Beast reared up, his pincers snapping viciously and slicing ever closer to the boy's head.

The medicine woman woke from her dream with a gasp. She sat upright, clutching her blankets, her heart hammering. A tiny scorpion lay at the bottom of her bed. She stepped out of the bed, her eyes never leaving the creature's glossy black body. The nightmare had just saved her life. Many Gorgonians had been found dead in their beds because a poisonous scorpion had found its way under the covers.

She pushed her way out of her tent. The boy's face was still clear in her mind. *Tom*. She had heard that name recently. Elenna had mentioned it. Tom was her friend.

Shivering, the old woman tried to shake off the feeling of dread that had crept over her. The dream felt like a sign of things to come. She'd had premonitions before. She hoped this one was wrong.

"Stay safe, Elenna and Tom," she muttered, gazing up at the swirling red sky of Gorgonia.

Scorpions were bad enough. A giant scorpion would be unstoppable.

CHAPTER ONE

DESTINY IN THE WEST

THE BLOODRED LIGHT FROM THE GORGONIAN sunrise peeped through the trees as Tom and Elenna made their way out of the forest, their faithful companions, Storm and Silver, ambling beside them. Vulturelike birds croaked on the branches overhead, and a thick mist lay on the ground.

Tom led the way, holding Storm's bridle. He noticed that Elenna kept her hand protectively on one of Silver's shaggy shoulders. The wolf had been badly wounded two Quests previously, and had only just returned to Elenna's side. Tom and his friends had already freed five of Avantia's

Beasts from Malvel's kingdom. Cypher the Mountain Giant was the last of the six Beasts being kept here against his will by the evil wizard. If they could free Cypher, their Quest would be complete.

Tom pulled his shield from his shoulder and studied the talismans set into its scarred wooden surface. The tokens from the good Beasts usually glowed and vibrated when a Beast was in danger. But Cypher's tear remained dark, and the shield had been still now for far too long. Where was Malvel keeping the mountain giant?

"Still nothing?" Elenna asked.

Tom shook his head. "It's as if Cypher is somewhere so far away that the shield can't sense him." He pushed his shield over his shoulder again, refusing to meet Elenna's eyes. He didn't want to reveal his worst fear: that he was already too late to save Cypher. "Perhaps the map will give us some clues," he said instead.

He took the smelly, worn parchment from Storm's saddlebag. Malvel had given them the map when they had entered Gorgonia for the first time. Each time they began searching for a good Beast, the map would give Tom a sign that he could use, or a green line would snake across its surface for Tom and Elenna to follow. Usually these signs and pathways would lead to trouble, but it was the only map that Tom and Elenna had.

"Nothing," Tom said, looking down at the map in disappointment.

"We can't trust it anyway," Elenna pointed out as Tom put the map away.

"You're right," Tom said. "I'll use my compass instead. It won't let us down."

Tom's uncle had given him the silver compass for his birthday. Instead of north and south, the words "Destiny" and "Danger" were inscribed upon its face. The compass had belonged to his father, Taladon, who was once the Master of the Beasts for Avantia and had disappeared when Tom was a baby.

Tom held the compass and walked in a complete circle. As he pointed it to the west, the arrow whirled several times and came to rest on Destiny.

Tom felt his heart lift. He put the compass away. "The compass is telling us to go west," he told Elenna. "I'm sure that's where Cypher is. While there's blood in my veins, I *will* find him and get him home to Avantia!"

Storm neighed and tossed his black mane as if he were agreeing. Silver sprang ahead down the path, eager to get going, and Tom and Elenna pressed on after him.

In the far distance, they saw something lying on the ground.

"What's that?" Elenna asked, shading her eyes in the red light.

Tom used the power of the magical golden helmet to bring the object into focus. Although the precious golden armor had been returned to Avantia at the end of the last Quest, he still possessed its gifts, and the helmet gave him extrakeen vision.

It was a boy, sprawled on the ground and riddled with arrows. His body was twitching. Tom felt his skin turn cold.

"It's Seth," he said to Elenna. "He's hurt."

Seth was one of Malvel's servants. Tom and Elenna had fought him before, and each time, the boy had been intent on killing them.

"Do we help?" Elenna asked.

Tom hesitated.

Seth was his sworn enemy. What should he do?

CHAPTER TWO

DARK SURPRISE

SETH SUDDENLY LET OUT A GROAN OF AGONY that echoed through the trees.

Tom knew what he had to do. He couldn't ignore another person in pain, even if that person was his enemy. To do such a thing would make him as bad as Malvel.

Tom tugged Storm's bridle, leading the black stallion toward the figure. Elenna walked beside him, with Silver pressed close to her side.

The path broadened and the trees thinned out to reveal a black, mirrorlike lake. Seth lay close to the water's edge. He was still breathing, but only just. His rib cage rose and fell in shallow gasps. Six arrows were embedded in his chest, and his blood had seeped onto the ground. It seemed impossible that he was still alive.

Tom was now close enough to see the beads of sweat on Seth's forehead. Storm dug his hooves into the path, then stepped backward. His nostrils flared.

"Hush, Storm," Tom said, soothing his horse.

"Silver doesn't like this, either, Tom." Elenna gazed down at her wolf. Silver's growls were deepening, and the hair was standing up on his back.

"Seth can't do anything to us," Tom reasoned. "Look at him. He needs our help."

He gave Storm's bridle to Elenna. Then he took hold of Epos the Winged Flame's feather and grabbed it from the front of his shield before kneeling down next to Seth. As gently as he could, he pulled three arrows out of the boy's body, and held the phoenix's feather to each wound. Seth's skin instantly began to knit together, and one by one the wounds began to heal.

Seth's groaning eased. His eyes fluttered open. Seeing Tom, he cried out in panic, "No! Leave me alone!"

Ignoring Seth, Tom pulled the fourth arrow from the boy's chest and healed the gaping hole.

Seth's eyes filled with terror. He began pushing Tom away, as his strength started to return. "You don't know what you're doing!" he gasped. "You should have left me to die!"

Tom ignored him. He took hold of the fifth arrow and pulled.

With surprising quickness, Seth grabbed Tom's wrist and pushed the arrow back into himself with a scream of pain. Tom heard Elenna gasp with horror. Storm whinnied and tried to pull away from Elenna's grasp, while Silver stood still, his tail between his legs.

Tom could understand why his friends were so spooked. It was almost as if Seth *wanted* to die.

Tom steadied his hands and swiftly pried Seth's fingers away from the arrow, drawing the dripping shaft out of the boy's flesh.

"No," Seth moaned, as Tom took hold of the sixth and final arrow. "Don't do it."

"Something is wrong here, Tom," Elenna said, shaking her head. "I think we should respect Seth's wishes and leave him."

"He's mad with pain," Tom reassured his friend. "There is just one more arrow. . . ."

Tom pulled the sixth arrow loose. Seth lashed out with his fists as Tom held the phoenix feather to the fifth and sixth wounds, but he was too weak to knock Tom's hands away. In an instant, his injuries had healed.

Seth let out an unearthly screech and writhed on the ground, making Tom jump back in alarm.

Elenna worked desperately to soothe Storm and Silver as they tried to turn tail and run.

Something was happening to Seth. Something awful . . .

They watched in horror as the boy's legs fused together, forming a single limb that lengthened and tore through his clothes. It grew darker and harder until it turned into a bulbous, beaded tail. The tail swiped out powerfully at Tom and Elenna, knocking them both to the ground.

Seth screamed again. His voice sounded deeper and rougher. Four legs forced their way out of both sides of his torso, tearing through his tunic.

"Get back!" Tom shouted to Elenna as they both got to their feet.

Seth sprang onto his new legs and let out a horrifying roar as two pincers burst from his stomach and began clicking and snapping in Tom and Elenna's direction. Tom could hardly believe what was in front of him. The bottom part of

Seth's body looked just like a scorpion, but his chest, arms, and head were still human. Seth pointed at Tom and Elenna, his face a mask of anger and despair.

"You!" he screamed, his voice terrifyingly deep. "This is your fault! This is Malvel's punishment for my failure. If you'd let me die as I wished, this wouldn't have happened. I wouldn't be a monster!"

With a roar of fury, Seth picked up his sword, which had been lying by the side of the path. Its wickedly serrated edge glinted in the bloodred light. With his giant scorpion pincers snapping, he advanced on Tom and Elenna.

CHAPTER THREE

THE BATTLE BY THE LAKE

"DON'T COME ANY CLOSER," TOM ORDERED, pointing his blade at the creature in front of him.

Seth gave a ghastly chuckle. His long tail reared high in the air, ready to strike.

"Tom," Elenna gasped, staring up. "Look!"

Tom followed her gaze. Something was gleaming at the tip of Seth's tail — a purple jewel. An amethyst. Instinctively, Tom touched the belt he wore around his waist — a belt already decorated with five jewels, each of which he had taken from the Beasts of Gorgonia. . . . If Seth had a jewel, it could mean only one thing.

"Seth's an evil Beast now," Tom whispered to Elenna. "The last one we must defeat."

"Enough talking!" Seth roared, lunging at them.

Elenna dove away, while Tom dodged to one side. He found himself next to the black lake that lay beside the path, and heard a rush of air as Elenna released her arrow. But the arrow bounced harmlessly off Seth's scaly tail.

Seth swung his sword above his head and sprang toward Tom. The Beast moved so fast that Tom had to use the magical power of the golden boots to leap into the air and avoid the vicious blade. The tip of Seth's sword missed Tom's stomach by a hair.

The momentum of the attack carried Seth to the edge of the lake, where he teetered for a moment on the bank, desperately struggling to stay upright. Then he looked down at his reflection in the black water, and Tom saw his enemy's face sag in horror.

"I'm hideous!" Seth screamed in despair, falling to the ground, away from his reflection.

Tom felt a surge of pity for the vile creature in front of him, but there were no words that could possibly comfort him. Tom turned and joined Elenna, who was standing with Storm and Silver. As he did so, a swirling red cloud dropped out of the sky and surrounded them. A tall wizard in bloodred robes stepped out of the scarlet mist.

"Malvel!" Tom gasped.

The Dark Wizard inclined his head. "The young hero," he said, a thin smile spreading across his face. "I knew your *good heart* would get you into trouble one day."

Tom realized now that this was all part of Malvel's plan. The wizard knew he would try to help the injured Seth. Angrily, Tom leveled his sword at him, ready to do battle. But with a wave of one thin hand, Malvel placed a shimmering, magical barrier in front of himself and Seth. Growling furiously, Silver hurled himself at the barrier but he bounced off the magical shield with a yelp, almost as if he had been burned by fire.

"I beg you, Malvel," Seth sobbed, collapsing before the wizard. "Turn me back to how I was!"

Tom saw the wizard look coldly at his servant. "Stop sniveling," Malvel commanded. "This is your punishment for failing me so many times. You are no longer to be called Seth, but Sting the Scorpion Man. And I command you, Beast, to go to the Western City of Gorgonia and guard Cypher the Mountain Giant."

Sting bowed his head in defeat. Malvel conjured a shining red orb from the air, which pulsed and grew in his hand. Then he threw it at Sting, imprisoning the new Beast in his bloodred heart.

Muttering in a language that Tom didn't understand, Malvel clapped his hands together three times. The giant red orb rose into the air, and, with a flick of his long, bony finger, Malvel sent it west toward the mountains. In an instant, the orb was out of sight.

The Western City. Tom gazed at the mountains on the horizon, committing them to his magical super-memory, a power he had won when he had defeated Narga the Sea Monster. The orb may have flown too fast for him to follow its exact path, but Tom felt sure that the Western City lay somewhere in those mountains.

He was torn from his thoughts by Malvel's cruel and cackling laughter.

"I know what you are planning," laughed the evil wizard. "But don't bother to follow Sting. There is no way that you will ever find Cypher."

With a final screech of laughter, Malvel wrapped himself in red mist and disappeared.

"He's wrong," Tom told Elenna fiercely, pulling himself into Storm's saddle. "We will find Cypher and we will get him home."

Elenna nodded, looking as determined as Tom felt. Silver nosed around her feet as she picked up the arrow she had fired at Sting. She then slung her bow over her shoulder and climbed into the saddle.

Tom gazed to the west, where two Beasts — one good and one bad — awaited them. "We're coming, Cypher," he whispered. "And we will never stop looking for you. Not while there's blood in our veins."

↠ CHAPTER FOUR ↞

THE VOICE IN THE WELL

THE FOREST PATH WOUND ALONG THE SHORE of the black lake, emerging onto a wide-open plain that ended at the line of black mountains where the red orb had disappeared. Grabbing Malvel's map, Tom found the Western City. But the map was playing a new trick, one that Tom had never seen before. The image of the Western City floated across the ragged parchment, shifting mischievously from one place to the next.

"The map is no good to us," Tom said. "All we can do is head through the mountains and hope to find the Western City for ourselves."

Elenna nodded, and they pushed forward.

Gradually the terrain grew rougher and the track narrowed as they approached the mountains. Tom rode Storm carefully, avoiding any sharp stones that might lame the stallion. Soon, the path disappeared completely, and they had to weave through stunted black shrubs and trees, whose twigs and branches caught at their clothes and whipped cruelly across their skin. The bloodred sun climbed higher, and the air was searing hot.

After half a day of moving through the arid heat, they found themselves back on a stony path, and Tom spotted a cluster of dull red towers in a cleft between two mountains. Tom took out Malvel's map and looked at the image of the Western City, which flitted across the map like a ghost. Its walls were red just like the towers he could see ahead.

"I think we've found the Western City," Tom said eagerly, reining in Storm so that the stallion could rest.

Elenna and Silver both sat down on the hot, dry ground. As Tom replaced the map in the saddlebag, he felt Storm's sides heaving. The stallion was panting heavily in the heat. Looking around, Tom saw a well a little farther on.

He pointed it out to Elenna. "Let's get some water," he suggested, and led Storm toward the well. Elenna and Silver followed close behind.

They leaned over the circular wall of the well and peered inside, hoping to see a long, dark shaft and the welcome glint of water at the bottom. But all they saw was a pile of rubble and loose stones. The sides of the well had collapsed inward, blocking it up completely.

Tom rested his head on Storm's sweaty flank. "I'm sorry, boy," he said. "We'll find some water soon, I promise."

Storm whinnied trustingly and pushed at Tom's shoulder with his velvety black nose.

"Perhaps there will be another well closer to the

city gates," Elenna said, shading her eyes from the glare of the sun as she stared up at the Western City. They were now a little closer, and the city's dark red walls gleamed in the sunlight.

"Hmm, I'm not sure that there are any more arou —" Tom broke off as the earth suddenly rumbled beneath their feet. Storm reared up, and Silver growled and retreated behind Elenna's legs.

"What was that?" Elenna asked nervously. "An earthquake?"

Tom felt a tingling sensation rush up his arm from his shield. Cypher's token was vibrating! The earth rumbled again. The movement seemed to be coming from the broken well. Tom leaned over the lip of the well and listened. The rumbling was an echoing roar. Tom recognized it at once.

"It's Cypher!" he cried.

The giant roared again. The ground shook.

"What is he saying?" Elenna asked.

Thanks to the ruby set into his belt, Tom could understand the good Beasts of Avantia. Now he sensed the giant's rage. "He's angry," he said, trying to explain the feelings that were running through him as he listened to Cypher. "He's trapped somewhere underneath the Western City. He can't breathe properly — he feels like he is choking."

"We have to get underground right away and help him," Elenna said determinedly.

"Maybe we can climb down the well shaft and look for some kind of underground tunnel that will take us into the city," Tom suggested.

Elenna nodded. "You'll have to move some of these rocks," she said. "I'll help as much as I can."

The golden breastplate had given Tom the gift of great strength. He seized the boulders that blocked the mouth of the well and heaved them aside as if they were feather pillows. Elenna took care of some of the smaller rocks. Before long, they had collected a pile of rocks and cleared a dark space in the well shaft. But the old walls of the well had relied for too long on the support of the boulders, and now they collapsed. They could no longer hear Cypher's voice.

"It's no good," Tom said.

"We'll have to head into the Western City." Elenna looked thoughtful. "I'm sure we'll be able to find a way underground once we're there."

"True," Tom said. "If a giant the size of five men can be taken underground inside the Western City, then there would have to be a very big trapdoor somewhere, right?"

"Right!" Elenna agreed.

Together, the four companions moved on along the scrub-covered track that led to the gates of the Western City.

Tom hoped he was right about the trapdoor. They didn't have much time — and Cypher's life was hanging in the balance. . . .

CHAPTER FIVE

THE GATEKEEPER

As THEY APPROACHED THE GATES, TOM FELT all his senses sharpening. He glanced around. From the time he and Elenna had arrived in Gorgonia, Malvel had put a price on their heads. Who knew how many bounty hunters were waiting among the rocks ready to capture or kill them? The closer they came to the city, the greater the danger became.

They won't catch us, Tom thought fiercely. *We'll fight to the death if we have to!*

The great red city loomed up in front of them. Its defensive walls towered overhead and were streaked with slime. Skulls were set into the brickwork, and evil-looking spikes lined the tops of the walls, their tips glinting in the red sun. The city's huge black gates were firmly closed. But there was no sign of any guards.

Silver growled uncertainly as Tom and Elenna stopped in front of the silent gates, and Storm pawed the ground anxiously.

Tom dismounted and gazed around. "Why are there no guards?" he asked Elenna.

"Perhaps it's a trap," Elenna replied uneasily.

There was a sudden movement from behind one of the trees that flanked the gates. A thin man in old brown robes, wearing a tattered eye patch and holding a walking stick, stepped out to stand before them.

Tom recognized him at once. "Kerlo!" he said.

"Hello," Kerlo replied. "If you wish it, I will let you into the city."

Tom wasn't sure that he trusted Kerlo, even though the Gorgonian gatekeeper had helped them more than once. Instinctively, his hand went to his sword. Elenna, too, held her bow and arrow at the ready.

Kerlo shook his head sadly. "Still so suspicious," he muttered. "Have I not been an ally on your Quest? Have I not aided you?"

"But why do you help us?" Tom challenged. "What's in it for you?"

Kerlo rested his weight on the long wooden stick that he held in his gnarled hands. "I was once a good wizard," he said quietly. "I tried to help the rebels in their fight against Malvel, but the Dark Wizard's magic was more powerful than I had ever imagined. He condemned me to spend an eternity as gatekeeper — between worlds." His face grew bleak. "I have not been able to cross a threshold in many years. I cannot even enter my family home." The gatekeeper fell silent for a moment. "You must understand, home is like a jewel, but it is only once it has gone that you realize how precious it is."

"We thank you for all you have done, Kerlo," Elenna said. "Will you help us get into the Western City?"

Kerlo nodded. "Once inside, you must head to Malvel's castle," he said. "In the castle's courtyard, you will find a trapdoor that leads to the cemetery that lies beneath the city. Those catacombs might be just the place to hide a giant Beast."

Kerlo held his hands out toward the gate. With a crash that shook the ground, the huge iron gates swung open. As they walked through them, Tom saw that the entrance to the city was set out in a series of three paths, just like the beginning of a maze. There were three possible routes into the city, but how could they be sure that they would choose the right one? And what would happen if they were wrong?

→ CHAPTER SIX ←

DANGER IN THE WESTERN CITY

TOM TURNED TO ASK KERLO FOR ADVICE. BUT the iron gates had already silently swung shut behind them, and the gatekeeper was gone.

Tom thought quickly, then pulled out his silver compass. He aimed it at the path on their right. At once, the arrow swung to Danger. Tom moved the compass until it pointed at the central path. The needle flew to Danger again, quivering slightly this time. Then Tom turned the compass to the last of the three paths.

For what seemed an age, the needle hovered uncertainly. Tom was about to put the compass back into his pocket when the needle swung slowly around to Destiny and held steady.

"This way," said Tom, tugging at Storm's bridle.

They moved cautiously down the path. Bloodred walls flanked them on both sides. Overhead, the red sun hid behind black clouds, casting long, bruise-colored shadows that seemed to bode ill. An archway loomed up ahead. Two Gorgonian guards were patrolling it, their weapons slung casually over their shoulders. Beyond the guards, Tom and Elenna could see a city square surging with strange-looking people, whose bodies seemed to be hunched and crooked.

"I think we need to try the direct approach," Tom whispered.

Elenna nodded.

"Hail!" Tom called out, taking Storm with him as he strode toward the guards.

"Who goes there?" called the first guard in a harsh, croaking voice.

"Two travelers," Elenna replied, coming to stand at Tom's side. Silver bounded up next to her.

The second guard narrowed his eyes. His gaze flicked to Storm and Silver, then back again. "What is your business in the Western City?" he growled.

"Rest," Tom replied, holding firmly on to Storm's bridle. "Food. Will you let us pass?"

The first guard looked as if he were about to step aside. But then the second guard jabbed his finger in Elenna's direction. His eyes were suddenly full of greed. "I know you," he said. "You're wanted by Malvel. Your faces are on posters all over this city!"

The game was up. Using the power from his golden boots, Tom leaped up and seized the guards around their thick necks, bringing their heads together with a loud *thunk*. The guards slumped unconscious to the ground.

"Take their cloaks," Elenna said, looking all around her. "We can disguise our faces with the hoods."

Quickly they stripped off the guards' cloaks and flung them over themselves. After adjusting their hoods to make sure that no one would see their faces, they walked through the archway with Storm and Silver at their side.

The city square was bustling with beings that didn't quite look human. Their eyes were yellow, and their hair grew in ragged patches. Scarred, spotty skin hung loosely off their faces, and their teeth were black and pointed. With a shudder, Tom noticed that their hands looked like claws. Keeping their heads down and holding tightly on to Storm and Silver, Tom and Elenna walked across the glossy black flagstones of the square.

Malvel's castle was impossible to miss. They could see it in the distance, on the fringes of the city. Forks of black lightning like huge lizard

tongues flickered in the red sky above the castle's turrets, and Tom knew at once that it was the center of all evil in Gorgonia.

The only way to reach the castle was to pass right through the center of the city. Tom hoped that their disguises would hold out that long. He could see several WANTED ALIVE posters displaying their faces, stuck here and there on the city's slimy walls.

"There isn't much trading or bartering going on, is there?" Elenna whispered, glancing from left to right as they hurried on.

Tom shook his head. It looked as if the creatures of the Western City seemed more inclined to fight and argue than trade. Noisy skirmishes were breaking out all across the square.

A fight exploded between two men just as Tom and Elenna were passing.

"Give me my money!" screamed a ragged-looking fur trader. "These are pure fox pelts!"

"Fox pelts?" his opponent roared back. "Cats, more like. You won't get any money from me!"

There was suddenly a whirl of fists and kicking legs, which Tom and Elenna managed to sidestep. Silver was not so lucky. The wolf gave a high-pitched yelp of pain as the fur trader's heavy-soled boot caught him in the ribs.

"Silver!" Elenna gasped.

Without thinking, she ran to her wolf's side and knelt down beside him. As she did so, her hood fell back, revealing her face.

There was a deathly hush in the square, followed by screams of recognition.

"Avantians!"

"Elenna!" Tom shouted, his own hood falling away from his face. "They know it's us! Run!"

CHAPTER SEVEN

MALVEL'S CASTLE

HORDES OF GORGONIANS LUNGED TOWARD Tom and Elenna, their scaly arms outstretched and their fists swinging. With his super-strength, Tom threw off each approaching attacker as easily as if they were rag dolls. Barreling through the angry mob, he cleared a path across the square. Elenna leaped nimbly onto Storm's back, and the horse lashed out with hard hooves while the Gorgonians tried to close in again. Elenna galloped after Tom, with Silver nipping fiercely at the ankles of any Gorgonian foolish enough to stand in their way.

Tom grabbed his sword and flashed it left and right in warning. Elenna then galloped close enough for him to seize a handful of Storm's mane and pull himself into the saddle. They broke free of the attackers and raced toward the castle. Storm's black tail rippled out like silk, and Silver was a blur of gray fur as he sprinted at their side.

As they approached the castle, Tom used his super-sight to check how many guards were on the gates. He didn't like what he saw. Two sentries were on patrol. Various weapons hung from their waists, and they each held a wicked-looking sword.

Keeping out of sight of the guards, Elenna turned Storm's head, and they raced into a copse of trees at the foot of the castle walls.

"We'll never get past them," Tom said, dismounting. "I'll send my shadow in to find an alternative route."

"Good idea," said Elenna, jumping from Storm's back.

The diamond that Tom had won when he had beaten Kaymon the Gorgon Hound had given him the gift of being able to send his shadow away from himself. However, Tom could not move while he and his shadow were separated. Tom and Elenna settled themselves behind a rock that gave them a good view of the castle.

"Go, Shadow," he ordered. "Find a way inside Malvel's castle."

Tom's shadow peeled away from him, slipping over rocks and between trees, until he could press himself up against the castle walls. The guards noticed nothing. Tom's shadow glided along the walls, feeling for any nooks and possible entrances with his thin black fingers.

"Anything?" Elenna whispered to Tom.

"Nothing yet," Tom said, standing absolutely still.

The guards' voices carried to where Tom's shadow was standing. Through his shadow's ears, Tom could hear that they were arguing.

"I'm leaving," one of the guards was saying. "You do what you want."

"But —"

"Our shift's over," said the first guard impatiently. "So what if the next guards haven't arrived?"

"We're supposed to wait till they get here. . . ."

The first guard snorted. "Wait all you like. I've got better things to do."

Hardly able to believe his luck, Tom watched through the eyes of his shadow as the first guard set off down the hill toward the city. After a moment's hesitation, the second guard followed. The gateway was clear.

Tom swiftly pulled his shadow back to him.

"Now's our chance," he told Elenna, jumping up into Storm's saddle. He held out his hand and helped Elenna up behind him. "Quick, before the replacements get here."

Storm burst out from the cover of the trees and galloped through the unattended gate into the castle's courtyard, with Silver just behind.

Tom and Elenna leaped off the stallion and gazed around in awe. Malvel's castle was built entirely of polished black stone, and streaked with gleaming stripes of red that pulsed like veins.

The trapdoor Kerlo had described was difficult to miss. It was so big it took up more than half of the courtyard.

"Just the right size for a giant," said Elenna grimly.

"Malvel must have taken Cypher down here," said Tom, walking over to where a huge iron ring was set into the trapdoor. "There's no other way he would have gotten him below the ground."

Storm whinnied and Tom glanced up at him.

"We'll have to take Storm and Silver with us," he decided. "It's too risky to leave them behind. The replacement guards will be here soon."

Kneeling down, Tom took the huge iron ring in his hands. He braced himself, and pulled.

Thanks to the great strength given to him by the golden breastplate, he was able to pull it easily, and the trapdoor opened with a gentle creak. A gigantic hole was revealed beneath it. Damp stone steps led down into darkness.

Tom lifted the huge door to shoulder height and rested for a moment. It was taking all of his strength to hold it.

"I'm going to have to push the door right open and let it fall," he said to Elenna. "Keep Storm and Silver out of the way."

"Won't that make too much noise?" Elenna asked, urging Storm and Silver back. "The guards will come running."

"We have no choice," Tom replied as he hefted

the door upward. "We've got to get down there and find Cypher."

He pushed the trapdoor all the way up, then let it fall backward to the ground with a thundering crash.

Tom could hear shouts of alarm from deep inside the castle. "Follow the steps down!" he yelled to Elenna, grabbing Storm's bridle. "The guards are coming!"

→ CHAPTER EIGHT ←

THE TOMBS

THEY RACED DOWN THE STEPS INTO THE yawning blackness of the tunnel. Tom yanked hard at the two long loops of rope that hung on the inner side of the trapdoor. Creaking and groaning, the door heaved slowly upward and then came crashing down into place. Tom, Elenna, and their companions crouched in the gloom and listened as guards ran into the courtyard above them. Their muffled voices drifted down through the trapdoor.

"What was that noise?" one said. "For a moment, I thought the master's castle was crashing down about our ears."

"Sounded like the trapdoor," grunted another.

Tom held his breath. What if the guards figured out that there were intruders underground?

A third guard scoffed. "The only way to open that door is with a team of men and some of the master's most powerful horses. It'll be the giant, no doubt, kicking and screaming belowground."

Tom felt Elenna tense at the mention of Cypher.

"He'll not be bothering us for much longer," said a fourth voice. "Come on — we need to find out what that noise was. Let's check the outer walls of the castle; maybe something has collapsed there."

Tom listened to the retreating footsteps as the guards left the courtyard.

"What did they mean about Cypher?" Elenna asked once everything was silent.

"I don't know, but time is running out," said Tom. "We need to move."

He looked around at the tunnel. There appeared to be only one path leading away from the trapdoor and it was lit by flaming torches. The walls were rough, and pools of water lay in puddles on the ground.

Tom, Elenna, and their animal companions raced through the twisting passageway, which sank deeper into the ground with every turn. The sides of the tunnel grew smoother as they ran on, and Tom noticed with a chill the tombs that had been set into the tunnel walls. He remembered Kerlo's words. These were the catacombs: the place where the Gorgonians of the Western City buried their dead.

As he ran along, he couldn't help but read the names on the tombs by the flickering torchlight: *Memnon, Arantis, Crestar, Xeropes* . . .

Taladon.

Tom stopped dead at the smooth black tomb bearing his father's name. His breath caught in his throat. Taladon wasn't dead. He was Malvel's prisoner. Wasn't he?

"Tom?" Elenna turned and came back up the tunnel to where he was staring at the black tomb. She held Storm's bridle tightly in one hand and Silver loped behind her, his eyes gleaming in the torchlight. "What's wrong?"

"I have to open this tomb, Elenna," Tom said fiercely, drawing his sword.

"There's no time, Tom," Elenna said. She seized his sleeve. "We have to save Cypher."

Tom shook off Elenna's hand. His father might be lying here, right in front of him! He took a step back and smashed the butt of his sword into the face of the tomb. The stone cracked. Tom slammed his sword into the stone several more times until it buckled, revealing a gaping black hole. But there was nothing inside. The tomb had never been used.

Elenna grabbed Tom's arm. "We have to hurry!"

Tom was about to reply when the ruby on his belt began to glow and his head was suddenly filled with Cypher's voice. The good Beast was telling him once more that he was finding it hard to breathe. Tom whirled around and stared down the tunnel. He suddenly understood. Cypher had been buried alive in one of these tombs!

Tom was filled with remorse. Why had he stopped to open Taladon's tomb? It had been a selfish thing to do, and now Cypher's life was truly in danger. Tom knew that he would never forgive himself if they were too late!

"Cypher is in real trouble," he said to Elenna. "I've got to go."

"Hurry, then. We'll catch up," Elenna replied.

Tom raced down the tunnel using the speed given to him by the golden leg armor, and left his friends far behind. The walls blurred around him — and the tunnel suddenly opened up. Tom skidded to a halt. He was in an underground chamber with a low ceiling. A massive tomb like a great stone mountain stood in the center of the room. A name had been carved in huge letters on the tomb's side.

Cypher.

Tom's head pounded. He could sense that Cypher was weakening. There wasn't a moment to lose. He pulled his sword from its sheath and smashed it repeatedly into the side of the tomb. The echo of steel against stone boomed around the chamber. But the stone of this tomb was much thicker than that of Taladon's, and even with his huge strength, Tom couldn't break the tomb open.

Then he spotted a ledge, just above the tomb. If he could just get onto it, he could then try to lever the tomb open with his sword. Tom thought rapidly. The golden boots gave him the power to leap great heights. He bent his legs beneath him, and jumped into the air, kicking off the giant tomb for an extra surge of height. With a thump, he landed on the stone ledge above the tomb. He then drew his sword and desperately started to lever up the lid.

Very slowly, it began to give. Tom worked hard, sweat pouring from his brow as he focused every drop of his magical strength on opening the tomb. At last, there was a gap wide enough for him to see into the tomb.

Cypher lay very still, as if unconscious. His one great eye was closed. He was breathing in short, shallow gasps. Tom could see that he was bound by two huge silver chains that crossed over and around his vast, shaggy body.

With one more massive push, Tom shifted the lid off of the tomb and stood on the side of the casket. He raised his sword above his head and brought it down on one of the chains that held

Cypher. But the blade bounced harmlessly away, the impact sending fierce vibrations up Tom's arms. He tried again and again, but he soon realized the chains were enchanted and would not break. Tom could feel despair threatening to overwhelm him. How was he going to free Cypher?

The sound of cantering hooves echoed down the tunnel, and Storm, Elenna, and Silver raced into the chamber.

"I can't do it, Elenna!" Tom panted, shaking his head. "My sword isn't strong enough to break the chains!"

"Don't lose hope, Tom!" Elenna shouted up to him. "Remember the gift of the golden chain mail? Strength of heart! You must believe in yourself. You must believe that you can do it!"

Tom lifted his sword shakily above his head. Closing his eyes, he concentrated with all his might. He could feel the magic of the golden armor pulsing in him. Bringing the sword down with a yell, Tom cut clean through one of the chains, which slithered away from Cypher's body like a silver snake. The mountain giant's eye fluttered open.

"One more blow, and you'll be free," he promised, and raised his sword for the second time.

But before Tom could bring his blade down, a hideous, jet-black tail came crashing through the chamber's wall. . . .

Sting!

CHAPTER NINE

TRAPPED!

TOM GRIPPED HIS SWORD TIGHTLY, READY TO fight, as the rest of the scorpion man's body smashed through the wall. How could he have forgotten? Malvel had sent Sting to guard Cypher. There was no way that he would let Tom free the mountain giant without a fight.

Fixing his gaze on Tom, Sting scuttled across the chamber toward him. He raised his pincers and clashed them together, the ghastly sound echoing around the rough stone walls.

"At last," Sting said in a voice that no longer held any trace of the boy Seth. "I will have revenge for all that you have cost me."

Tom knew he had to find some extra strength to fight Malvel's last Beast. Everything depended on it.

He sprang from the edge of the tomb and tumbled through the air, landing squarely on Sting's back. With a roar, the Beast thrashed his tail and the amethyst at the end of it just missed Tom's eye.

With lightning speed, Sting spun around. Caught off balance, Tom fell to the ground. He pulled his shield from his back and flung it over his head as a giant pincer sliced toward him. The pincer bit into the edge of the sturdy shield as if the wood was made of butter.

"Over here, Sting!" Elenna yelled, distracting the Beast as she drew back her bow and aimed an arrow.

"Leave us, girl," Sting said roughly. "This is not your battle."

"If your battle is with Tom, then it's with me,

too," Elenna retorted, releasing her arrow. It hit the Beast's stomach, but his skin was like armor there, and the arrow bounced off, falling to the ground. Sting roared in annoyance and turned to Elenna.

Tom staggered to his feet, eager to protect his friend, but Silver got there first, racing in to bite at Sting's scaly legs. Storm also cantered forward and reared up, lashing out at the Beast with his hooves. Sting snapped his pincers like scissors, slicing at Storm's mane.

Tom felt a surge of pride as he saw his friends bravely fight the Beast. At the same moment, he heard a rattling sound from the tomb. Cypher was struggling against the second silver chain. His strength was returning! Tom gripped his sword tightly; he knew he needed to deal with Sting before he could free the good Beast.

Tom called Storm and Silver away from the scorpion man, while Elenna let loose another arrow. This time, it embedded itself in Sting's neck, which was still soft and human. With a screech of pain, Sting flung his hand to the arrow and tried to pull it out. It gave Tom the chance he had been looking for. He raised his sword and charged forward, ready to strike at Sting's heart.

But Tom wasn't prepared for the Beast's powerful tail. It flew toward him like lightning. Tom just managed to avoid being crushed by its weight, but the amethyst at the tail's tip cut deep into his cheek.

Tom could feel the warm blood trickling down his face. He looked up to see Sting's tail coming toward him again. With a surge of anger, he whirled his sword and swung it upward, slicing the tip of the tail clean off.

Sting screamed, the sound shaking the walls. The tip of his tail flew across the chamber and hit the floor in a spurt of black blood. The amethyst came loose from its setting, rolling across the chamber floor toward Elenna. She bent down and snatched it up, sharing a triumphant glance with Tom. They had the final jewel!

Tom could hear Cypher still struggling to free himself from the second silver chain as Sting turned on Elenna, mad with pain. Tom tried to get past the Beast's injured tail, but even without its tip, the tail was still powerful and knocked him to his knees every time.

Suddenly, there was a crash from the tomb. Tom whirled around.

"Cypher!" he shouted joyfully. "You're free!"

The mountain giant had managed to pull himself away from the second chain. With a roof-shaking roar, he climbed to his feet and pounded on his chest.

The chamber walls trembled and fragments of rock cascaded from the ceiling as Cypher's head brushed the roof. The giant roared again, kicking away one side of his tomb, which fell to the floor with a mighty crash. The foundations of the chamber shuddered, and part of a wall crumbled into a heap. The movement of Cypher's huge bulk was putting massive strain on the catacombs. The whole place looked and sounded as if it were about to crash down on top of them!

Sting backed away from Elenna with a snarl, his eyes flickering around the disintegrating chamber before he turned and scuttled down the tunnel toward the trapdoor.

Cypher bellowed loudly, raising his arms. Tom could feel the good Beast's wild delight at being free. More rock began to fall to the ground.

"There's no time to lose," Tom called to Elenna. "We have to follow Sting, and get out of these tunnels before everything collapses!"

Narrowly avoiding a shard of rock that speared into the ground beside him, Tom grasped a handful of Storm's mane and pulled himself into the saddle. Elenna jumped up behind him.

They began to gallop up the tunnel after Sting. Cypher lumbered after them, with Silver running alongside him.

Straining every muscle, Tom guided Storm between the crashing boulders that fell like giant black hailstones. Tombs smashed to the ground, spilling their bones into Storm's path. Grimly, Tom pushed on up the steep passageway. In the flickering light, he could see pools of sticky black scorpion blood on the ground. Tom knew that they had to catch Sting before he got to the trapdoor. He had no doubt that the Beast planned to leave them trapped in the collapsing chamber. Tom reminded himself that Sting had lost a lot of blood and would be getting weaker. There was still time to stop him.

The tunnel began leveling out, and ahead Tom could see Sting scuttling up the great stone steps toward the trapdoor. With what little strength he had left, the Beast heaved open the hatch and pulled himself out of the hole.

Tom leaped off Storm and sprung forward.

But he was too late. With a resounding *thud*, the scorpion man slammed the trapdoor shut. The torches that lit the catacombs sputtered in the draft, and went out.

Cypher, Tom, Elenna, Storm, and Silver were plunged into shaking, rumbling darkness.

CHAPTER TEN

PURPLE MIST

OVERHEAD, TOM COULD HEAR STING ORDER-
ing guards to place Malvel's enchanted bolts into
the trapdoor. The sound of hammering started up
immediately.

"I'm going to try to push the door open," Tom
said, feeling his way up the stairs.

"Good luck," Elenna replied anxiously.

Tom tried with all his might to heave open the
trapdoor. But it would not budge.

Then Cypher gave a roar and lumbered up the
stairs to help. Together, Tom and the mountain
giant pushed at the trapdoor with all their
strength.

"Be quick, Tom," Elenna said. "This chamber sounds as if it is going to collapse at any moment."

"It's no good," Tom panted, disappointment flooding through him. "Whatever enchantment Malvel has put on the bolts, it is too strong."

Tom felt Cypher's frustration rush over him like a wave.

"What are we going to do?" Elenna's voice trembled in the darkness. "There must be another way out."

The ground shook beneath their feet. The shuddering tunnel walls threatened to cave. In that instant, Tom wished more than anything that he could be home in Avantia.

Kerlo's words suddenly echoed in his mind. "*Home is like a jewel,*" the gatekeeper had said. "*But it is only once it has gone that you realize how precious it is.*" Had the gatekeeper been trying to give him some kind of clue?

"Do you still have Sting's jewel, Elenna?" Tom asked, leaving the stairs and feeling his way along the tunnel toward his friend.

There was a bloom of purple light as Elenna pulled the amethyst from her pocket. Tom took it carefully and held it up in front of him. The light began to pulse. Then Tom felt his hand move through the air, drawing a doorway in the darkness with the edge of the jewel. With a rush of delight, Tom realized that the jewel was cutting a magical gateway that would get them out of the catacombs.

Far above them, Tom could hear Malvel's castle groaning and crumbling. The collapsing catacombs must have damaged the very foundations of the castle.

"Stand close to me," Tom commanded, as more rocks fell around them.

His hand was still moving, the jewel drawing the last part of the new gateway. The darkness peeled away in a sharp, clear line. Beyond the freshly cut door, a purple mist swirled and beckoned.

"Tom," Elenna gasped, her eyes shining as she clasped Tom's hand. "Do you think this will take us back home to Avantia?"

"I hope so." Tom hardly dared to believe that they were just a step away from their beloved homeland. In his mind he called to Cypher, telling the good Beast to follow them through the gateway. Then he seized Storm's bridle, while Elenna grasped Silver's scruff, and together they dove into the cool purple mist.

The air stretched. Tom felt himself spinning. Bright lights glowed all around him.

"Good-bye, Tom and Elenna. . . ." Kerlo's voice echoed all around them.

Tom started to say thank you to the gatekeeper but an awful scream, full of fury, interrupted him. It was Malvel.

"You have not seen the last of me, Tom," Malvel screeched. "I will be victorious!"

But just as the words left Malvel's mouth, the wizard suddenly gave a shriek of fear. Tom could hear the sound of tumbling, crashing rock, and then nothing more.

Tom sensed the massive bulk of Cypher spinning beside him. Then the giant seemed to disappear, and Tom, Elenna, Storm, and Silver landed on the familiar floor of King Hugo's throne room, where the King and Wizard Aduro were waiting for them.

"Welcome home," Aduro said, smiling and holding out his hands in greeting. "I knew you would prevail, Tom. You have defeated Malvel once again and, although I could not see as clearly as I would have liked, I believe that the Dark Wizard was crushed beneath the rubble of his own castle."

Tom felt a wave of relief surge through him as he embraced Aduro, but this was quickly replaced with panic. Where was Cypher? Had the giant somehow been pulled back into Gorgonia?

"The giant has returned to his rightful place — in the mountains," said King Hugo, sensing Tom's worry. He rose from his throne. "Well done, Tom. You are truly Avantia's greatest champion."

Tom bowed his head. While the King thanked Elenna for all her help, Tom looked out of one of the throne-room windows. The sky was sapphire blue, and the sun shone gently down on the green land that surrounded the castle. Brightly colored flags and pennants fluttered from the houses in the distance. They had escaped the swirling red fog of evil Gorgonia forever.

"We are holding a feast in your honor in the Great Hall today," King Hugo announced, as he stroked Storm and Silver in turn. "Avantia is impatient to welcome home her heroes."

A servant walked in and draped a soft woolen blanket over Storm's back, before leading the stallion away for food and a warm stable full of fresh straw. Tom looked down at the amethyst that still lay in his hand. He slipped it into his belt. The row of six jewels glowed fiercely, filling the throne room with a rainbow of light and power.

King Hugo clapped an arm around Tom's shoulder, and Aduro walked between Elenna and Silver. Together, they all moved toward the palace stairway and down to the bustle of the Great Hall below, where the feast was being laid out. Brightly suited servants carried groaning trays of food, and musicians tuned their instruments in the minstrels' gallery. The citizens of Avantia were already streaming through the palace doors in their finest clothes, and the air was buzzing with chatter and laughter.

As Tom took his place at the top table between King Hugo and Elenna, his thoughts strayed to Malvel and Seth, the boy who had turned into a Beast. Had they really perished in the ruins of the castle? Then he thought of Odora and the Gorgonian rebels he had helped to escape into Avantia on his Quest to rescue Tusk the Mighty Mammoth. Where were they now?

Shaking the thoughts from his head, he turned to Elenna and raised his glass. "Here's to the completion of another Quest," Tom said. "I couldn't have done it without you, Elenna."

Elenna clinked her glass against Tom's, and with her other hand fed some chicken to Silver, who sat at her feet. "You are welcome, Tom," she said cheerfully. "But why don't you smile? Malvel is gone at last and it's all thanks to us!"

Tom drank deeply from his goblet, then grinned at his friend. He would allow himself to smile today — but only time would tell whether they had seen the last of Malvel!

WILL TOM BE REUNITED
WITH HIS FATHER?

BEASTQUEST®

AMULET OF AVANTIA

→ BOOK NINETEEN ←

NIXA
THE DEATH BRINGER

BEASTQUEST

AMULET OF AVANTIA

NIXA THE DEATH BRINGER

SCHOLASTIC

AN ALL-NEW QUEST BEGINS!